TIGER TALES

Priya Sehrawat

ISBN
Paperback 979-8-89906-649-8
Hardcase 979-8-89906-846-1

*"I know there's a magic forest somewhere,
I know there's some magic everywhere."*

CONTENTS

Chapter – 1

THE ADVENTURE BEGINS

"We're finally doing this!" Priya exclaimed, her eyes lighting up as the car sped down the winding country road. Her excitement was over the roof, her fingers tapping lightly on the dashboard as the jungle landscape thickened around them.

"Yeah, and in typical Priya fashion, you dragged us into the middle of nowhere," Siddharth teased from the driver's seat, his focus half on the road and half on the spirited conversation going on beside him.

Kritika, seated in the back, chuckled as she leaned forward. "I still can't believe my parents agreed to let me come with the two of you! Who'd have thought I'd be going on a trip with no adult supervision!"

Siddharth beamed with confidence as he replied, "Ugh... excuse me... I am eighteen years old! Besides, you'll be an adult in a matter of months."

"Ugh... excuse me... I'm a good seven months older than you..." added Priya with a smirk before turning to Kritika,, "Since my dad's friend Bill is also visiting the resort with his wife... he reassured my parents that we'd be well looked after. And then my parents spoke to Siddharth's parents who spoke to your parents... and..."

"We know, we know…Uncle Bill and Aunty Margaret from Australia!" Siddharth mimicked Priya in an attempt to tease her.

"Hey! They are fun to be around. You'll see!" she replied, eager to meet her dad's old friends.

"But I bet neither of our parents read those internet reviews. They were kind of sketchy." said Kritika with concern in her voice.

"Sketchy is an understatement! Did you forget about the tourists that went missing only six months ago? They said the tigers ate them whole." said Siddharth in a playful tone.

"What? I didn't know any of that!" replied Kritika in shock.

"He's teasing you!" said Priya nudging Siddharth on his shoulder.

"You should have seen the look on your face!" laughed Siddharth as he took a slow turn on a rather narrow path.

Kritika gave Siddharth a cold stare and continued in a serious tone "I just wonder how safe this resort is," she said, squinting her eyes to see beyond the dark forest canopy.

"Safe is boring!" Priya exclaimed. "We're here for the adventure, right? Besides, the legends about the tiger deity and the village's mysterious history... don't you find it fascinating? There's something magical about this place."

Siddharth smirked, glancing over at Priya. "You and your magic. Just don't go chasing after something in the jungle."

Priya leaned back, ignoring the light-hearted jabs. "I've read stories about these jungles. Baghpore was famous a hundred years ago for its tigers. The locals believed there was magic protecting the village, keeping the tigers here. Then the British hunters came and the magic disappeared." Her eyes sparkled with the thrill of the unknown. "You'll see. There's something about places like this... you can feel the energy. It's ancient, it's powerful."

Siddharth laughed. "You've been watching too many fantasy movies. This is just a remote tiger reserve. It used to have tigers a hundred years ago, and now it's trying to attract tourists again. Simple."

"I wouldn't call it simple," Kritika added in a cautious tone. "I mean, this place was shut down for years. Tigers disappeared. People stopped coming here. Now suddenly, there are tiger sightings again? Feels… weird."

Priya smiled. "Exactly! The locals used to worship the tiger deity, and the magic kept the tigers here. Maybe it's returning. You never know."

Siddharth sighed, his eyes narrowing as the road stretched on ahead. "Whatever this 'magic' is, let's just make sure we don't end up being part of some local legend, alright?"

The road narrowed even further as they neared their destination. The GPS announced they had arrived, though there was no visible sign of a resort, only a dirt path leading into the trees.

"Uh, are you sure this is the place?" Kritika asked furrowing her brow as she peered out the window.

The sky was now streaked with purple and orange as dusk settled in and the jungle grew darker by the minute.

"This has to be it," Siddharth said, slowing the car. "Priya's dad said it's remote... maybe too remote." He pulled the car onto the dirt path, its wheels bumping over uneven terrain.

The path opened up into a clearing, and there it was, The Baghpore Tiger Resort, a sprawling, old-world structure, half-hidden by the thick foliage around it. Lanterns lit up the front, giving it a warm glow against the encroaching night. The air was thick with the sounds of the jungle - crickets, distant bird calls, and the faint rustle of leaves in the breeze.

Priya bounced in her seat. "Oh my god, I love it already! This is exactly the kind of place where something mysterious could happen."

"Okay, that looks... nicer than I expected," Kritika admitted, her voice soft with surprise.

Siddharth parked the car, and they stepped out. The rich, earthy scent of the jungle filled their nostrils. Priya stretched her arms wide, taking a deep breath. "This is going to be incredible!"

They were greeted by an overly cheerful staff member as they approached the entrance. The man smiled widely as he bowed. "Welcome, welcome! It's a pleasure to have you here at our humble resort."

Priya beamed back at him. "Thank you! We've been looking forward to this."

The man nodded enthusiastically. "We'll make sure your stay is unforgettable…" he said as he picked up their luggage. "Isn't he a bit too happy?" muttered Siddharth only to be dismissed by Priya "It's his job!" she hissed before giving a wide smile to the man.

As they walked through the resort, the charm of the place began to unfold. The narrow stone path wound gently through the trees, lined with lanterns that looked like glowing fireflies in delicate glass cages. Fragrant blooms spilled over trellises, their sweet perfume mingling with the earthy scent of moss and woodsmoke. They passed by numerous small luxury cottages, each one uniquely adorned and bearing its own whimsical name. "The Moonlit Grove," "The Whispering Pines," and "The Secret Garden" were just a few that caught their attention.

They reached their own cottage, nestled among the trees, named "The Enchanted Retreat." The exterior was painted a soft, welcoming blue, and intricate wood carvings adorned the door. As they stepped inside, the warm glow of lanterns greeted them. The interior was a blend of rustic charm and modern luxury, with plush furnishings, handwoven rugs, and large windows that offered a view of the surrounding gardens.

"Oh wow," Kritika breathed, her initial fear and confusion evaporating like morning mist. "This is incredible!"

The walls were lined with local artwork, and fragrant candles flickered on the mantelpiece, casting dancing shadows around the room. A small kitchenette boasted fresh fruits and artisanal snacks, and a cozy seating area with a large, inviting sofa beckoned them to relax.

"I could live here forever," Priya said, wandering deeper into the cottage.

"Let's not get carried away," Siddharth replied with a grin. "We're only here for the weekend."

They quickly changed into cleaner clothes, leaving behind the travel grime.

"Aren't the two of you hungry?" Kritika asked, glancing at the glowing lights outside.

"Absolutely," Priya said, her eyes gleaming with excitement. "I can't wait to see what they have for us!"

As they walked towards the dining area, a short, stocky man with a nervous expression hovered nearby. His eyes darted around as if he was looking for something, or someone.

Soon, he found the courage the approach them.

"Excuse me, are you three heading to dinner?"

"Yes, we are," Siddharth replied with a hint of curiosity and caution in his voice.

The man took a deep breath and glanced around before he spoke. "I…I'm Pinto. Just wanted to offer a bit of… friendly advice. The jungle around here… it's not like other places." His voice was low, as though he didn't want to be overheard.

Siddharth raised an eyebrow. "What do you mean by that?"

Pinto hesitated, his eyes anxiously surveying the surroundings. "The tigers. They've... been acting strange lately. There's been more activity than usual. Just... be cautious on your safari tomorrow. You never know what might be lurking."

Priya grinned. "More tigers? That's what we came for, right?"

Pinto didn't return the smile. "People come here for the tigers, but they forget…these animals are wild. They don't follow rules. And sometimes… people don't come back." He cleared his throat and stepped back, giving them a stiff nod before walking away.

Kritika watched him leave, her forehead creased. "That was... unsettling."

Priya waved it off. "He's just trying to scare us. You know how people love telling ghost stories about these kinds of places. We'll be fine."

Siddharth, ever the practical one, gave a small nod. "We'll be careful, though. Just in case. No wandering off on your own, Priya."

"I don't wander off... much," Priya teased, lightening the mood.

As they waited for their food to arrive, Kritika couldn't shake the strange feeling that Pinto's words had left behind. "Do you think he was just trying to spook us, or was that an actual warning?" she asked quietly, falling into step beside Siddharth.

Siddharth shrugged. "Hard to say. Ugh, excuse me?" He called out to a passing waiter, "Hey, do you know anything about a guy named Mr. Pinto? He just warned us about the tigers."

A wide grin spread across the waiter's face as he chuckled softly. "Ah, Mr. Pinto! He loves a good scare. You see, he's a local who owns a wood factory just outside the village. With all the tourism rising, his business has taken a hit, so he tries to scare the tourists away." He shrugged, waving his hand dismissively. "We've tried to keep him off the property, but he somehow keeps sneaking in."

"Thanks for the tip," Siddharth replied, though the waiter's explanation didn't quite ease the knot forming in Kritika's stomach. As the waiter walked away, she turned to Siddharth. "Do you really think Pinto was just playing games?"

"Seems like it," Siddharth said, although a trace of doubt lingered in his tone. "But it's always good to be cautious, right?"

Priya laughed lightly. "Oh come on, guys! It's probably just a local legend to keep tourists on their toes. I'm sure the tigers here are used to seeing people. Let's not overthink it."

Kritika sighed. "Maybe you're right."

"Yes!" exclaimed Priya, looping her arm across Kritika's shoulder. "Tomorrow's going to be awesome. We're going to see tigers, have fun, and it'll be an adventure we'll never forget."

The three friends tried to shake off Pinto's odd warning but the unease lingered as they settled into their cozy cottage, each retiring to the three tiny beds lined up next to one another. The sounds of the jungle grew louder as night fell. Kritika couldn't help but feel as if the night was watching them, waiting for something to unfold, but the company of her friends put her at ease, as she slowly drifted off into a deep slumber.

Chapter – 2

THE SAFARI

The next morning came quickly as the jungle woke up with the first hints of dawn. The air was cool and fresh, and the sky was a soft gray as clouds began to gather in the distance.

Kritika stirred awake, the distant sounds of the jungle were alive, a symphony of chirps, rustles, and the occasional call of a bird echoing in the morning air.

She looked around, and much to her surprise, neither Priya nor Siddharth were anywhere to be seen. A sense of fear and worry came upon her as she was immediately reminded of Mr. Pinto's warning. Reluctant, she got out of the bed, tiptoeing her way to the bathroom. She knocked on the bathroom door, whispering "Priya…Siddharth… any of you in there?"

Kritika waited, her heart pounding in her chest as silence stretched on, broken only by the persistent calls of the jungle outside. Just as she was about to knock again, the door behind her swung open.

"Good morning, sunshine!" Priya bounced into the room, her hair a wild halo around her face. "We have a safari to catch!"

Kritika jumped back, nearly tripping over her own feet. "Priya! You scared the life out of me!" She placed a hand over her racing heart, trying to catch her breath. "Where have you been? I thought something happened."

"Oh, come on! It's a beautiful day!" Priya spun around the room enthusiastically. "Siddharth and I went for a quick walk to check out the gardens. You wouldn't believe how many flowers there are! We found a little path that leads deeper into the jungle, but we didn't go too far."

Kritika's eyes widened. "You went into the jungle? Alone?"

Priya waved her hand dismissively. "It's fine! Besides, I wanted to see if I could catch a glimpse of the tigers. But we didn't see any," she added, her tone shifting to a playful pout. "Just a bunch of colorful birds and some monkeys swinging through the trees. You really should have joined us!"

Siddharth appeared behind her, ruffling his hair as he entered the room. "And you should have seen Priya trying to talk to the monkeys! I swear she thinks they understand her."

Kritika shook her head, her worry dissipating slightly but still lingering at the back of her mind. "You guys should be more careful. Remember what Mr. Pinto said? We're in a wild jungle, not a petting zoo!"

Priya rolled her eyes but stopped her twirling to give Kritika a serious look. "I know, I know. Now, let's get ready quickly, we just have half an hour before the safari begins."

"That reminds me," Kritika continued "where's your uncle Bill and his wife? I thought they were joining us soon enough."

"They said they'll be here in-time for the safari." replied Priya.

"I am sure we'll see them soon, provided we leave on time." said Siddharth pointing at his wrist watch.

"Remember, we're sticking together," he reminded them as they gathered their essentials - a camera, a pair of binoculars, and a small first-aid kit. "No wandering off, and definitely no petting any tigers."

As they stood outside the resort, waiting for the safari jeep, an elderly couple approached them.

"Priya!" a sturdy, broad-shouldered man called out. He seemed to be in his early sixties, with tanned, weathered skin and a silver-streaked beard. He wore a khaki shirt, cargo pants, and a wide-brimmed hat, clearly used to the outdoors.

"Uncle Bill! How lovely to finally see you" said Priya, giving him a warm hug before spotting Margaret approaching them.

"Aunty Margaret!" she exclaimed, running towards her.

"She's… delighted…" said Siddharth with a chuckle.

"Aye, seems that way…" replied Bill. "We haven't seen her since she was twelve.! Oh by the way, I'm Bill, and that is Margaret. We're from Australia, flew in only yesterday!"

"We know," said Kritika with a warm smile, "Priya has told us all about your adventures with spiders in Australia."

Bill seemed to be getting ready to narrate one of his adventure stories before getting interrupted by his wife.

"Lovely to meet you young folks!" Margaret said cheerfully. She was tall and poised, had ash-blonde hair tied back in a scarf. Dressed in a white cotton shirt and khaki pants with binoculars around her neck, she looked calm, curious, and ready for adventure. "We've been coming to India every couple of years, and this is our first time here at Baghpore. Bill's been talking about tigers for months!"

Bill chuckled. "Oh yes, India's on quite a few bucket lists back home. The wildlife, the culture… It's all so different and exciting. I've read about these jungles since I was a boy."

"We'll be lucky if we spot a tiger, but let's hope today's our day," he added, tipping his hat with a wink.

The group was joined by a man named Rajan. Bill introduced him as their personal guide. He had a sturdy build and carried a calm, reassuring presence.

"This group keeps getting larger, with the jeep nowhere in sight" muttered Siddharth.

"The more, the merrier!" Kritika grinned, nudging Siddharth's arm. "Besides, an extra pair of eyes might help us spot a tiger."

"That's the spirit!" said Priya, delighted at her friend's optimism.

A few moments later, a rusty open jeep pulled up in front of them. The engine sputtered before settling into a steady rumble. It was driven by a young, quiet man with a strong jaw and dark, watchful eyes. Seated next to him was their forest guide, a local named Shailesh who greeted them with a warm smile.

"Good morning, everyone. The jungle's been lively these past few weeks. We're hoping today's no different," Shailesh said as he motioned for them to take their seats.

As they set off, the jungle around them came to life. The sound of birds calling from every direction filled the air, and the thick trees, intertwined with vines and dense foliage, created a sense of adventure. Kritika, far from her usual suspicions, seemed mesmerized by the scenery.

"This is unreal," she said, leaning out of from her seat. "I mean, just look at this place! It's so wild and untamed."

Priya nodded excitedly. "I know, right? There's something so raw and beautiful about it. Today's the day, I can feel it."

"Aye, I can feel it too!" Bill added, giving his wife a quick grin.

As the jeep ventured deeper into the jungle, the clouds overhead began to thicken. The once-soft gray turned a menacing dark blue, and a heavy breeze stirred the leaves.

"Looks like rain is on its way," Siddharth commented, peering up at the sky.

Shailesh nodded. "We'll try to reach the more secluded areas quickly. Tigers are usually more active before a storm."

However, the weather didn't hold off. Within moments, a sudden downpour hit, turning the dirt path beneath the jeep into a slick, muddy trail. The rain was heavy, relentless, and soon, visibility became almost impossible.

"We might need to stop for a bit," Shailesh called over the pounding rain. "Too risky to drive in this."

The driver brought the jeep to a halt under a tin shed, offering some shelter from the rain. Shailesh and the driver exchanged a few quiet words before he climbed out of the vehicle.

"I'll be back shortly," said Shailesh. "Need to send a message to the front post to keep a safety vehicle ready, in case we get stranded out here."

"Can't you send it from right here?" asked an annoyed Margaret, as drenched as she could ever be.

"No signal in this spot, I need to go a few meters ahead. Just stay here, I won't be long."

"Wait, what if the Tiger just wanders off right here?"

"Wouldn't that be a treat?" chuckled Bill only to be stared at by his fearsome wife.

"In this rain? Not a chance! It's probably hiding somewhere, away from the rain, just as you are."

As moments turned into minutes, the rain fell heavier with no sign of Shailesh.

"I am going to go look for him," said the driver, and jumped out of the jeep before anyone could respond.

After a good half an hour, neither Shailesh nor the driver returned.

"Is this normal?" asked Margaret, looking over at Rajan, who sat beside her.

Rajan adjusted his cap and gave a slight nod, his voice steady. "Well, I'm no safari expert, but don't worry. We're in good hands. Sometimes drivers need to walk ahead to check the tracks or signal to each other, especially if there's a blockage or fresh signs of a big cat."

Bill looked around, a little uneasy. "Still, half an hour's a long time in tiger country."

Rajan smiled faintly. "That's true. But silence is part of the jungle's rhythm. The moment you think nothing's happening, something usually is."

"How long does it take to send a signal?" Kritika asked, her earlier excitement dimming slightly. "It's been a while."

Priya glanced around but shrugged it off. "They probably just found some cover from the rain. It's pouring out there."

"I don't know," Siddharth said, frowning. "This doesn't feel right."

The uneasy silence stretched on. As time passed, the distant roar of thunder rolled through the jungle.

Margaret shifted in her seat, her eyes narrowing as she gripped Bill's arm. "Did you hear that?"

"Hear what?" asked Bill, looking around.

"I'm sure I heard a growl," said Margaret, clutching onto Bill's arm. Rajan shifted in his seat too, suddenly unsure of the safety of his customers and his own.

"I didn't hear…" Kritika began, but her voice trailed off as another, more distinct growl followed.

Bill cleared his throat, his calm demeanor faltering. "We should probably head back to the resort."

"They wouldn't just leave us here, right?" Kritika asked, her earlier enthusiasm replaced with growing concern. "Maybe we should wait a little longer."

"I think Bill's right," Siddharth said firmly. "It's not safe to sit here. We need to head back."

Priya, however, was less willing to give up. "Come on, let's not panic. They'll be back soon, I'm sure of it. Shailesh knows these jungles like the back of his hand."

"Maybe," Kritika said slowly, glancing around nervously. "But I think we should leave too. Something feels off."

Rajan nodded, his decision made. "We're heading back." He reached over to the driver's seat, turning the key to restart the jeep.

The engine sputtered to life… but the wheels didn't budge. They were stuck deep in the mud, the tires spinning helplessly as Rajan tried to force them forward.

"Are you kidding me?" Kritika muttered, her voice rising in panic.

Bill stood up slightly, peering over the side of the jeep. "Looks like we're bogged down. Gonna need to give it a bit of a push."

"In this rain?" Kritika asked, her voice wavering now. "What if the tiger's close?"

"We don't have much of a choice, love," Margaret said, her face pale but determined. "Sitting here isn't doing us any good."

"I'll get down and push," said Rajan as he jumped down, "Bill, why don't you take the wheel." "Aye... I would... But I don't know how to operate these manual cars you've got inIndia!" said Bill with a sheepish smile."I'll drive!" said Siddharth enthusiastically.

He jumped into the driver's seat and hit the pedal while Rajan pushed against the rear of the jeep. The tires spun in place, spraying mud everywhere but refusing to gain traction. The group watched with a mix of tension and helplessness. Then, out of the corner of Priya's eye, something shifted in the bushes.

"Siddharth," she whispered urgently. "Siddharth, look!"

Her voice was barely audible over the rain, but the terror in her tone was enough to make heads turn. There, in the thick bush, two glowing green eyes stared back at them. For a moment, everything was still. The world seemed to hold its breath.

Then, with terrifying speed, the tiger pounced towards them.

It was a blur of orange and black, a massive beast that moved like lightning. The tiger leaped at Rajan, who barely had time to turn. It landed on him, digging its claws into his back as it dragged him into the jungle before anyone could react.

"Rajan!" Priya screamed, her voice cracking as the horror unfolded in front of them.

Kritika froze, her breath catching in her throat, her wide eyes locked on Rajan's vanishing figure.

Margaret, her face drained of all color, clutched Bill's arm. "Oh my God... oh my God, Bill!" sshe gasped as her eyes welled up with tears. Bill's usually calm face had turned ghostly white, and his mouth hung open in disbelief.

"We have to leave now!" Siddharth roared, fumbling to restart the engine. His fingers trembled as he turned the key, his usual composure shattered by the chaos. The engine whined and sputtered but refused to come to life, the tires spinning helplessly in the mud.

"It's not working! It's stuck!" he shouted. His eyes darted wildly around, searching for any sign of movement in the shadows, knowing full well the tiger could still be lurking, waiting for its next strike.

"What do we do? What do we *do?*" Priya's voice was frantic, her eyes darting between the treeline and the malfunctioning jeep.

"Rajan..." Kritika whispered, her body trembling violently. "It…it took him... we have to help him…"

"We can't help him!" Siddharth snapped, his face contorted with fear and anger, "He's gone. We have to get *ourselves* out of here before…"

A low, rumbling growl pierced the tension. The sound reverberated through the jungle. The tiger had disappeared into the shadows with Rajan, but they all knew it was still out there, watching.

Siddharth's hands shook as he twisted the key again and again. They were trapped, vulnerable, and the jungle around them felt suddenly too small. Too dangerous.

The growls echoed once more, louder this time, and Priya grabbed Kritika's arm in sheer terror.

"We have to go. We have to get out of here, now!"

Chapter – 3

THE RIVER CROSSING

The growls of the tiger still echoed in their ears as Siddharth slammed his foot on the gas. The jeep lurched forward spraying mud everywhere. But this time, it moved. Siddharth took a u-turn and drove back the same way they had come. The jungle around them blurred as they sped away, leaving behind Rajan's helpless memory.

"Oh my god… oh my god," Kritika mumbled, her voice trembling as she gripped the sides of the jeep.

Priya sat frozen, her wide eyes locked ahead as the trees whipped past them. She was usually the brave one, but now, even her adventurous spirit was cracking. "We have to get back. We have to find someone," she muttered, her voice shaking.

"We're not stopping until we get out of this damned jungle," Siddharth said, his jaw clenched with determination in his eyes. The rain pounded against the windshield, and the windshield wipers barely made a dent in the downpour. The jungle around them seemed endless, like they were driving in circles.

Bill and Margaret were silent in the back, their eyes wide with shock. The horror of what had just happened hung thick in the air. Everyone was too scared to speak. But their silence didn't last long.

"Look!" Bill shouted suddenly, pointing ahead.

Siddharth's heart sank as the jeep screeched to a stop. In front of them, the road ended at a river, swollen and raging with the torrential rain. The water rushed past, high and fast, its surface churning with white foam.

"No way... there's no way we can drive through that," Kritika whispered.

"We have to try!" Priya said urgently, though her voice lacked its usual confidence.

Siddharth shook his head. "The jeep will get swept away. We'll have to swim."

Bill's face paled. "We'll never make it across. That current looks vicious."

Margaret clutched her husband's arm, her eyes wide with fear. "Bill... we'll drown."

Siddharth took a deep breath. "We don't have a choice. It's either this, or we stay here and hope that the tiger doesn't come for us next."

Without another word, Siddharth jumped out of the jeep, the rain instantly drenching him. The others followed, though fear was etched on each of their faces. The river raged in front of them, but they couldn't stay where they were. Siddharth led the way, wading into the cold, swirling water. The current tugged at his legs, almost pulling him under immediately.

"Hold on to each other!" he shouted as the others followed him into the river.

Kritika was next, grabbing Siddharth's arm tightly as they fought the current. Priya held onto Kritika, her breath shallow as she felt the water dragging her down. Bill and Margaret struggled at the back, their faces filled with panic as the river surged around them.

Step by step, they waded deeper into the river, the current threatening to pull them under at any moment. Finally, after what felt like an eternity, they reached the other side, gasping for breath as they collapsed onto the muddy riverbank. The rain still fell in sheets around them, but for a moment, they were safe.

"Bill... where's Bill?!" Margaret cried, her voice breaking as she looked around frantically.

Kritika's eyes widened in horror as she realized the truth. "He's gone," she whispered.

Margaret screamed in disbelief "No! No, he can't be gone!"

Suddenly, a distant scream echoed through the jungle. Bill's voice, desperate and terrified, somewhere far off in the distance. "Help! Margaret!"

"Bill!" Margaret screamed, her face pale with terror. She sprinted into the jungle, her hysterical cries growing fainter as she disappeared into the trees.

"Wait!" Priya shouted, jumping up to run after her. Siddharth and Kritika scrambled to their feet, following close behind.

But the jungle was thick, the rain-slicked leaves and vines slowed their progress. The trees loomed large, their branches tangled in a mess of shadows, and within minutes, Margaret's figure vanished into the darkness ahead.

"Margaret!" Siddharth yelled, his voice cutting through the rain-soaked air. But there was no answer.

The group stopped, panting and drenched, looking around in growing panic. Margaret's frantic screams had faded into nothing, and now the jungle was eerily quiet, save for the soft patter of rain.

"We've lost her," Priya gasped, her chest heaving as she bent over, trying to catch her breath. "She's gone."

Siddharth's face was grim. "We can't go any further into the jungle. We'll get lost too."

"But we can't just leave her!" Priya cried, her voice rising in frustration. "She's out there, and uncle Bill…"

"Bill's gone, Priya," Siddharth said sharply, his voice filled with regret. "And now Margaret is too."

Priya fell silent, tears mixing with the rain on her face as she realized the harsh truth. There was nothing they could do.

The three of them stood there for a moment, drenched and exhausted, the weight of their situation sinking in. They were alone now, with no way of knowing what had happened to Bill and Margaret, and no clear direction to go.

"We need to keep moving," Siddharth said quietly, his voice heavy with the responsibility of leading them. "The longer we stay here, the more dangerous it gets."

Kritika nodded, though fear flickered in her eyes. Priya hesitated, her gaze lingering on the dark jungle where Margaret had disappeared, but finally, she too gave a small, reluctant nod.

With night falling, they had no choice but to press on, leaving behind the screams and shadows of the past few hours. Unaware of a way out of the jungle, they trekked deeper within it. The path grew less clear, overgrown with vines and thick underbrush. Hours seemed to stretch endlessly, and soon they found themselves disoriented, unsure of where they were heading.

"We're lost," Kritika said, her voice barely a whisper.

Siddharth didn't answer, but the grim expression on his face said it all.

"Look," Priya said suddenly, pointing ahead.

Through the trees, barely visible in the dim light, was the crumbling outline of an ancient structure. As they moved closer, the full sight of it came into view - ruins, overgrown with moss and vines, towering pillars that had long since fallen into disrepair. It was an ancient temple, hidden deep in the heart of the jungle.

"What is this place?" Kritika asked, her voice hushed in awe.

Priya's eyes sparkled with curiosity despite the fear in her heart. "I don't know... but it looks old. Really old."

"We should keep moving," Siddharth said, glancing warily at the temple.

But Priya stepped closer, her hand brushing against the worn stone. "This might be our best chance to find shelter for the night. At least it's safer than being out in the open."

Kritika hesitated, but finally nodded in agreement. "I hate to say it, but she's right. We need to rest."

Siddharth frowned but knew they had no other options. The jungle was unforgiving, and nightfall had already swallowed them whole.

Chapter – 4

THE TEMPLE

The ruins of the temple loomed above them, its ancient stones covered in moss. The night sky was barely visible through the thick canopy of trees, casting shadows that danced ominously around the crumbling structure. The once-grand carvings on the walls had faded, but even in their dilapidated state, the images of a tiger, a powerful deity, were still clear. Its eyes seemed to follow them, glowing faintly in the dim light.

"This place gives me the creeps," Kritika muttered, hugging her arms to herself.

"It's incredible," Priya whispered in awe, her voice barely audible as she trailed her fingers over the worn carvings. "Look at these... It's like the whole temple was built in honor of the tiger deity. They worshiped it."

Siddharth glanced around, his jaw set in determination. "We should stay focused. We still don't know what happened to Bill and Margaret."

But just as the words left his mouth, a noise cut through the air – footsteps. Slow, deliberate, and getting closer.

"Someone's coming," Siddharth hissed, pulling Priya and Kritika toward a dark corner of the temple. They crouched down behind a stone pillar, their hearts pounding in unison as the footsteps drew nearer.

A moment later, a group of figures entered the temple. At first glance, they looked like resort staff, but something was off. They were dressed in traditional, tribal attire - robes made of animal skins and beads, faces painted with markings that gave them a fierce, ritualistic appearance.

And then, to their horror, Priya, Siddharth, and Kritika saw them…Bill and Margaret.

The elderly couple was tied up, gagged, and dragged into the temple by the resort staff. Bill's face was pale, his eyes wide with fear, while Margaret struggled weakly against her restraints, her sobs muffled by the gag.

The three friends exchanged terrified glances, trying to remain as silent as possible.

One of the men, tall and muscular with a fierce scowl, began to remove the gags from Bill and Margaret. Bill's voice, hoarse and strained, broke the silence. "Why are you doing this? What do you want from us?"

The man who had removed the gag nodded to his companions, who gathered around the altar. Another man, shorter and with a more nervous demeanor, answered. "It's a tradition. Every month, we offer a sacrifice to the tiger deity to ensure our business thrives. The deity protects us and ensures the jungle remains a place where tourists will come."

Margaret's eyes widened with horror. "A sacrifice? But why? We're just ordinary tourists!"

The taller man continued, his voice cold and unfeeling. "The tiger deity demands it. Nature is unpredictable and dangerous. The sacrifices appease the deity, ensuring prosperity for the resort and safety for those who live here. No one questions the occasional missing person. The jungle claims them."

Bill and Margaret's faces were etched with terror as the truth sank in. Priya's hands shook as she clutched Kritika's arm, her mind racing with the implications. This was not just a remote temple, it was a place of ritualistic sacrifice.

The men finished tying Bill and Margaret to the altar and began to leave. One of them paused at the door, looking back for a moment as if checking everything was in place. Then, with a heavy creak, they pulled the massive wooden doors shut, sealing the couple and the three hidden friends inside the temple.

For a few seconds, the silence was deafening, broken only by the distant drip of rainwater leaking through the cracks in the roof.

"We have to get them out of here," Siddharth whispered, his voice low but urgent.

They waited a few more moments, listening carefully to ensure the men were gone, and then slowly emerged from their hiding spot and hurried toward Bill and Margaret.

"We're going to get you out of here," Priya said in a hushed tone. But just as they took a step forward, a loud cracking sound filled the air. Margaret and Bill's eyes widened in shock and terror as the floor beneath them began to shift. Before anyone could react, the stone beneath them gave way, sending both Bill and Margaret plunging into a dark abyss below. The ground closed up behind them with a final, ominous thud, leaving no trace of the gaping hole that had swallowed them.

Priya screamed, her voice echoing through the empty temple. "No! Not again!"

Siddharth and Kritika were stunned, frozen in shock as they stared at the now solid floor where the couple had vanished.

"We have to find another way," Siddharth said, "We can't just leave them here. There has to be another exit or a way to get down there."

"But where do we start?" Kritika's voice was shaky as she looked around the temple. The walls were covered in faded, cryptic symbols that seemed to mock their desperation.

"Let's search the temple," Priya said, her voice resolute despite her trembling hands. "There has to be some kind of clue or hidden passage."

They began to search the temple frantically, their hope and fear mingling in the dim light. Every corner, every hidden crevice, every forgotten artifact was examined in the hope of finding a way to rescue Bill and Margaret.

As they worked, the temple seemed to close in on them, the oppressive weight of its dark history pressing down with every passing second. The flickering light from their torches cast long shadows on the walls, making the carvings of the tiger deity seem to come alive, its eyes glowing with a menacing light.

The night stretched on, and the three friends continued their search, knowing that time was running out and that their own lives might be in danger as well. The secrets of the temple were deeper and more dangerous than they had ever imagined, and the jungle outside seemed to watch with silent, knowing eyes.

"What if the deity actually took them?" Kritika suggested, her voice tinged with unease. "What if it's not just a story?"

Priya, always inclined toward the mystical, nodded thoughtfully. "Maybe the magic is real. Maybe there's something we don't understand about this place."

Siddharth, ever the skeptic, shook his head. "There has to be a logical explanation. This is all too convenient. There must be another way out, another explanation for all this."

Priya's attention was drawn to the massive image of the tiger deity that dominated the far wall. The mural was unlike anything she had ever seen. It depicted the tiger standing proudly over a group of worshippers, its eyes glowing with power. There was something about it... something that drew her in.

"Priya," Siddharth urged, his voice sharp. "We don't have time for this."

But Priya was transfixed. She stepped forward, her eyes locked on the image as if in a trance. "There's something about this place..." she murmured, her fingers brushing against the stone wall beneath the mural. The stone was cold, but there was an energy to it, a strange, ancient power that pulsed through her fingers.

"Priya!" Siddharth nudged her by the arm. "Come on! Snap out of it!"

But before Priya could respond, the ground beneath her feet shifted.

The stone floor creaked ominously, and before any of them could react, the ground gave way. With a deafening crack, the floor beneath Priya and Siddharth crumbled, sending them plunging into the darkness below.

Kritika let out a scream as they disappeared from view, the ground collapsing into a hidden catacomb beneath the temple. The sound of their fall echoed through the chamber as they tumbled into the depths.

"Priya! Siddharth!" Kritika shouted, rushing to the edge of the hole. But all she could see was darkness, an endless void where the floor had once been.

For a moment, there was nothing but silence. Then, from the depths below, Kritika heard a groan of pain.

"We're okay," Siddharth's voice called up, "We're... down here."

Kritika's heart pounded as she peered down into the darkness. She could barely make out their forms, crumpled at the bottom of what appeared to be an ancient tunnel system beneath the temple. The air down there was thick and musty, and the faint sound of water dripping echoed through the cavern.

"Hang on," Kritika called, her voice trembling. "I'm coming to get you."

"No, no! You wait up there, keep an eye out. We'll find a way to come back up."

"Ugh...I'm not sure guys...I think we should all stay together and in sight."

"Don't worry, just stay hidden, we'll find a way up, I promise!."

Chapter – 5

THE SECRET UNDERGROUND

The air below was thick with the musty smell of old stone and decay. Priya and Siddharth scrambled to their feet, their breath coming in sharp, anxious bursts. The faint glow of their torches revealed a labyrinth of narrow tunnels, walls slick with moisture and lined with ancient, cobwebbed stones.

"What is this place?" Priya whispered, her voice trembling slightly as she peered into the oppressive darkness.

The sound of approaching footsteps echoed faintly through the tunnels, sending a shiver down their spines. Without a second thought, Priya and Siddharth darted into a shadowy alcove, pressing themselves against the cold stone wall.

Two figures emerged from the darkness, speaking faintly.

"I think they're coming this way," Priya whispered.

Siddharth strained to listen, trying to make out the conversation. His face lit up with recognition. "They're talking about a 'project', some kind of a smart city."

Priya's confusion was evident. "A city? What do you mean?"

Siddharth's brow furrowed in concentration as he tried to make sense of their conversation. "They're talking about cutting down the trees... they're going to remove the jungle… this 'project'… it's a plan to build a smart city here." ...but the locals are against it... seems like these people are trying to turn the public against the jungle!"

The realization hit them both like a jolt. The disappearances, the mysterious deaths, it all made sense now. As the men continued their conversation, they mentioned something about "preparing for the shipment" and ensuring everything was "in place for the next phase."

Priya's heart raced. "We need to find out where they're keeping Bill and Margaret. Let's follow them."

The two men walked ahead, unaware of their pursuers. Priya and Siddharth crept quietly through the tunnels, keeping their distance while straining to hear any further details. The twists and turns of the underground maze seemed endless, but they pressed on, driven by the need for answers.

Finally, the men came to a large, heavy door, which creaked open to reveal a dimly lit room filled with an array of screens and equipment. As the two men made their way out of a smaller door, shutting it behind them, Priya and Siddharth tip-toed through the heavy door. Inside, the walls were lined with monitors, each displaying live footage from different locations: the jungle, the resort, and the temple. The scene was almost surreal, a stark contrast to the decaying tunnels outside.

"What is this place?" Priya asked, her eyes wide with shock.

Siddharth's gaze was fixed on one particular screen. It showed a digital model of a tiger, its image flickering in eerie green light. A small, green chip was embedded in the model's head. "What's that supposed to be?" Priya said, thinking out loud.

"They're controlling the tiger," he said slowly, his voice filled with horror. "That chip... it's used to control its movements." "What! How do you know that?" "Well, all those sci-fi movies I see... it's always a chip in the brain that makes someone go bonkers!" "Movies?!" Priya hissed, "You can't e serious Siddharth! This is no movie, this is real!" "I know, I know. But look around you, it all makes sense!"

Priya stared at the monitor, trying to make sense of Siddharth's theory. "You mean the tiger is being used to hunt people? The 'magic'... is it just a cover for this?"

Siddharth nodded grimly. "It looks like it. The tiger's movements are being directed from here. They are using it to carry out the killings and making it seem like a wild animal attack."

The full scale of their discovery hit them with overwhelming force. The tiger, once a symbol of power and mystery, had been twisted into a tool of manipulation and murder. The resort's mysterious disappearances and the so-called sacrifices were all part of a sinister scheme to turn the public against the jungle and gather support for a smart city to be built in its place.

"We need to figure out how to stop this. Where will the wildlife go?" Priya whispered urgently.

Siddharth nodded. "First we need to get out of here. Let's find a way to disable the control system and get out of here before they notice we're gone."

They began to search the room, looking for anything that could help them. Siddharth's eyes were drawn to a large console in the corner, filled with buttons and switches. He approached it carefully, trying to decipher its functions.

"This looks like the control panel for the tiger," he said, pointing to the console. "If we can shut it down, we might be able to stop the tiger from being used against us."

Priya nodded, moving next to Siddharth, trying to make sense of the complex array of controls. They were interrupted by a sudden noise from outside the room; a heavy, metallic clank followed by voices.

"We have to hurry," Priya urged, her voice tense. "They'll be back any moment."

Siddharth worked quickly, his fingers flying over the controls as he tried to disable the system. The screens flickered and the digital model of the tiger jerked as he managed to sever the connection between the chip and the control panel.

"I think it's working," Priya said, her voice filled with hope. "The tiger should be free of their control now."

Just then, the door to the room burst open, and the two men from earlier rushed in, their eyes widening in shock as they saw Priya and Siddharth standing by the console.

"What are you doing here?" one of the men shouted, his voice filled with rage.

Priya and Siddharth exchanged a frantic glance. They had to escape, there was no time to explain or defend themselves.

As the men advanced, Priya grabbed Siddharth's arm and pulled him toward the door. They sprinted through the labyrinthine tunnels, the sounds of their pursuers growing fainter behind them. After what seemed like an eternity of running and hiding, they finally emerged into open air, the jungle night enveloping them once more.

"We have to find Kritika...the temple...where...how do we find it?" muttered Priya in confusion.

They looked directionless through the dark canopy of the forest. Their minds were filled with a tumult of emotions, fear for Kritika, anger at their predicament, and a desperate resolve to rescue the jungle.

Chapter – 6

THE RITUAL

Priya and Siddharth moved cautiously through the dense jungle, their feet cracking on the thick carpet of leaves. The sounds of the night filled the air with the distant calls of animals and the whispering wind through the trees. But something else caught their attention, a rhythmic chant that grew louder as they walked towards it.

"Do you hear that?" Priya whispered.

Siddharth nodded, motioning her to follow. "Let's check it out," he said quietly, his curiosity outweighing his sense of caution.

They crept forward, pushing aside the heavy vines until the forest suddenly opened into a wide clearing. A large bonfire crackled in the center, sending sparks high into the night sky. Around the fire was a group of men swayed in circles, singing chants in a strange language. The flames illuminated their faces, casting eerie shadows as they performed the ritual, completely unaware of the two spectators hiding behind the bushes.

Priya crouched lower, eyes wide as she took in the strange scene. "What are they doing?" she whispered, her breath visible in the cool night air.

Siddharth's eyes darted between the dancing figures and the glowing bonfire. "This must be some kind of ritual... maybe connected to the tiger deity," he murmured. "But...do you think they know about the secret underground? Or the smart city project?"

Priya shook her head. "I don't think so. Look at them, they seem to be taking this ritual pretty seriously. Maybe we should tell them!" raising her voice rose slightly.

"Shh!" Siddharth hissed, grabbing her arm. "No, we don't know how they'll react to us telling them that their beliefs are nothing but a cover-up for some tech villains! We have to be careful. What if they decide to sacrifice us as well?"

A moment of eerie silence followed. Siddharth froze, his eyes narrowing. "Wait... why is it suddenly so quiet around here?" he whispered.

Priya's heart skipped a beat. Slowly, they both looked up to find a group of tribals hovering above them, their spears pointed directly at the two helpless friends. The moonlight glinted off the sharp metal tips, and before Priya could collect herself, a loud scream escaped her mouth.

The tribals wasted no time. They grabbed Priya and Siddharth, pulling them from the bushes and dragging them toward the bonfire. Both of them kicked and struggled, but it was of no use. Their hands and legs were bound tightly, and they were forced to kneel in front of the roaring fire. The flames crackled loudly, casting an ominous glow on their terrified faces.

A tall, broad-shouldered man approached them, his face partially obscured by the flickering light. As he stepped closer, Priya's eyes widened in recognition. "It's him," she whispered urgently to Siddharth. "It's Shailesh!"

"Stay back!" Siddharth warned, trying to sound brave despite the spear just inches from his chest. He tugged at the ropes around his wrists, but they held firm. Priya's struggles beside him were equally futile.

Shailesh smiled deviously, as if admiring his new prey. "I'd hoped the Tiger would get you and your troublesome group at once but I guess it wasn't hungry enough!"

"Not to worry" said another man from behind. As he stepped closer, his face became visible.

"You…You were driving our jeep!" said Siddharth angrily.

The men exchanged amused looks but before they could speak, a loud roar echoed from the bushes. A flash of yellow and black streaked from the undergrowth, and the tiger leaped into the clearing. In one swift motion, it pounced on the Shailesh, knocking him to the ground. The tiger's powerful jaws clamped down on his neck.

Chaos erupted as the men scattered in every direction, running for their lives. The bonfire flickered wildly as the tiger, its mouth dripping with blood, lifted its head and locked eyes with Priya and Siddharth. They were left helpless, easy prey in front of the massive predator.

As the tiger took a step closer, its eyes glowed in the firelight. Priya's heart pounded so loudly that she was sure the tiger could hear it.

"Don't move," Siddharth whispered, his voice barely audible, but his words seemed to aggravate the tiger. It growled low and menacingly at Siddharth, as if displeased with his suggestion.

Siddharth froze, his body stiff with fear, certain that the beast would lunge at him any second. But then, something strange happened. The tiger turned its gaze back to Priya. She stared into its eyes, and for the first time, she noticed something unusual - its eyes. They weren't the usual deep green as before; they were golden, shining like two molten suns.

A strange sense of calm washed over Priya. The fear that had gripped her moments before was replaced with a surreal tranquility as she gazed into the tiger's golden eyes. Suddenly, thick smoke began to fill her vision. She blinked, but instead of seeing the fire and jungle around her, she was transported into a vision with a field, green and lush. In the distance, she saw a tiger playing with its cub. They rolled in the grass, the cub playfully batting at its mother's tail.

"What a happy moment," Priya thought, her lips curving into a soft smile. But the vision quickly shifted. A gunshot rang out, and the mother tiger fell to the ground. The cub whimpered beside her, its tiny body trembling in fear. Another crack, and a stun gun hit the cub. Gloved hands reached out, taking the cub away.

The vision shattered with a scream, pulling Priya back into the present. Her eyes widened as she watched the tiger in front of her being electrocuted by a metal wire, collapsing to the ground with a pained roar.

"No!" Priya screamed, struggling against her bonds. "Don't hurt him!"

"Priya! Siddharth!" A familiar voice called out, and Kritika emerged from the bushes, rushing to their side.

"Are you okay?" she asked, quickly working on the ropes binding Siddharth's wrists.

"The tiger… it's dead!" Priya cried, her voice thick with emotion.

"No, it's not." A stern voice cut through the night. Mr. Pinto stepped forward, emerging from the shadows behind the tiger. "It's unconscious, not dead. For now." He pulled a gun from his pocket, his face hardened with resolve.

"NO! Don't shoot him!" Priya yelled, her voice filled with desperation. She struggled wildly against the ropes as Kritika worked to free her. "You don't understand! This tiger isn't a man-eater! It's being controlled!"

Mr. Pinto frowned, clearly unconvinced. "It's a killer. It needs to be put down before it gets any more blood on its cursed mouth."

"No, Mr. Pinto, you don't get it!" Priya pleaded, looking to Siddharth for help. "Tell him, Siddharth! Tell him about the chip!"

Siddharth, now free from his bonds, grabbed a nearby spear and stood. "She's right, Mr. Pinto. It's not the tiger. It's the chip they put in its brain. They're controlling it, using it to attack people. There's much more going on here than you realize."

Mr. Pinto's laugh was incredulous. "A chip in a tiger's brain? You kids have quite the imagination."

"It's not our imagination!" Priya shouted, her anger boiling over as she stood. "We can show you! There's a control room in the temple. You have to believe us!"

Before Mr. Pinto could respond, the sound of footsteps approached rapidly. Siddharth's eyes widened in fear. "It's those men!" she whispered. "Hide!"

In an instant, the group dove into the bushes, remaining perfectly still as they watched the clearing. After a tense moment, a group of armed men wearing black uniforms entered. They circled around the unconscious tiger pointing their guns at it.

As Priya, Siddharth, Kritika, and Mr. Pinto watched in silence, two figures stepped out of the shadows. Dressed in white lab coats, a man and a woman approached the tiger, their faces cold and clinical.

"Is it dead?" the woman asked sharply.

"No, ma'am," one of the guards replied. "Only unconscious."

"Oh, my poor baby," the man said softly, kneeling next to the tiger and stroking its neck.

The friends and Mr. Pinto watched in stunned disbelief as the man fearlessly stroked the massive predator. The tiger let out a soft whimper, and the guards tensed, ready to shoot at any sign of danger.

"Careful, sir," one guard warned.

The man chuckled. "He'd never hurt me. After all, I'm his father," he said as he rose, his voice tinged with a twisted sense of pride.

"Now, where's the remote?" he asked. The woman handed him a small black device, which he pointed toward the tiger. But before he could press the button, the tiger began to stir, its body twitching as it regained consciousness.

The tiger let out a low, menacing growl as it stood, looking around in confusion. The guards hesitated, guns at the ready, but the man raised his hand.

"Nobody shoots!" he commanded. "I have it under control."

Just as the tiger prepared to leap, the man pressed a button on the remote, and the tiger immediately calmed, sitting in an attentive position.

Mr. Pinto and Kritika exchanged looks of complete disbelief.

"Alright, kitty," the woman said dismissively. "Let's get to work."

"Don't insult him!" the man snapped. "Come on, boy," he said, patting the tiger on the head before walking away, the tiger obediently following him.

Priya, Siddharth, Kritika, and Mr. Pinto were left in the bushes, their minds reeling from what they had just witnessed.

Chapter – 7

THE CONNECTION

The jungle loomed dark and ominous as the four huddled together behind the thick bushes, still shaken by what they had just witnessed. The sight of the man controlling the tiger with a remote, as though it were nothing more than a puppet, weighed heavily on their minds.

Mr. Pinto found me at the temple... he... he told me... "said Kritika glancing over at Pinto, hinting him to continue." I work for the Jungle Security Agency, and I was sent her to investigate thedisappearances." "Well, you have no idea what Priya and me have discovered." said Siddharth.

"What could possibly be going on here?" Kritika asked,

Siddharth shook his head, the disbelief evident in his eyes. "Whatever it is, it's bigger than we thought. That man... he's behind the deaths, I'm sure of it. He's using the tiger as a weapon. They're killing tourists."

Priya nodded, her face pale. "They Plan to clear the jungle and build a smart city out here. The mysterious deaths, the disappearances... they've all been orchestrated by him. The tiger's just a tool to turn the public against the jungle."

Mr. Pinto rubbed his chin thoughtfully, his eyes narrowing as he processed the information. "This is darker than I imagined. We need to get somewhere safe before they realize we know too much. I have a hideout… a small watchtower on the edge of the jungle. It's hidden, and we can send out a signal for help from there."

Siddharth glanced around the jungle warily. "We need to move quickly. If they find us before we reach your tower, we're done for."

Nodding in agreement, the four of them set off into the jungle, moving silently but swiftly through the thick underbrush. As they walked, Priya fell into step beside Siddharth and Kritika, her face a mix of uncertainty and determination.

"I need to tell you both something," Priya began, her voice low. "Back there, when the tiger looked at me, I saw something… strange. I felt this connection, like it was trying to show me something."

Kritika looked at her with concern. "What do you mean? What did you see?"

Priya took a deep breath, recalling the vivid vision that had flashed before her eyes. "It was like I was transported to another place. I saw a tiger playing with its cub in a field. But then the vision turned dark. The mother tiger was shot, and the cub was taken. I think that man's been doing this for a long time. And somehow, I feel like the tiger isn't just an animal to him. It's connected to something deeper, something… personal."

Siddharth's eyes widened as he listened, a new urgency building in his voice. "The tiger is a victim as well. What kind of people are they? How can someone in their right senses do something so evil?"

Priya nodded, her expression resolute. "Yes. We can't just let that man use it for his twisted plans. We have to save the tiger along with Bill and Margaret."

Kritika reached out, placing a hand on Priya's shoulder. "We'll do everything we can to stop them, Priya. We're in this together."

Siddharth nodded. "We'll find a way to stop that man and save the tiger. But first, we need to figure out where they're keeping Bill and Margaret."

Mr. Pinto, walking slightly ahead, overheard their conversation and turned back to them. "I have a theory about that," he said grimly. "Years ago, I was part of an undercover mission in Serbia. There was a lab conducting illegal experiments, putting chips in animal brains to make them more efficient, more obedient. The government shut it down, but I always suspected it wasn't the end of the story."

Kritika's breath hitched. "You think the man and the woman we saw have some connection to that lab?"

"It's possible," Pinto said, his eyes scanning the dark jungle. "I've seen people like them before - scientists willing to go to any lengths for their experiments and capitalists willing to use technology for their own benefit. But we'll only know for sure if we survive long enough to find out."

As the group neared the edge of the jungle, the tension in the air grew thicker. Soon, in the distance, the silhouette of a tall, rickety structure came into view - It was Pinto's hideout.

"There it is," Pinto said, relief creeping into his voice. "We're almost there."

But Kritika suddenly froze, her eyes darting around the shadows of the trees. "Wait... do you hear that?"

The others stopped, listening intently. The jungle, which had been filled with the hum of insects and rustling leaves, now felt unnervingly silent. And then, a familiar sound - a deep, menacing growl echoed through the trees.

"The tiger!" Priya whispered, her heart racing.

Without another word, the group broke into a run, sprinting toward the tower as fast as they could. The growls grew louder, and behind them, the rustling of leaves signaled the tiger's approach.

"Faster!" Siddharth yelled, his breath ragged as the tower came closer into view.

Kritika and Siddharth reached the tower first, leaping onto the ladder and scrambling up with all their might. Priya and Mr. Pinto followed, but as they reached the base of the ladder, Pinto stumbled and fell to the ground with a groan.

"Pinto!" Priya cried, rushing to help him up. "Come on, we have to move!"

Pinto managed to get back on his feet, and they pushed toward the ladder. But just as he started to climb, the tiger lunged from the shadows, its massive body crashing into him with terrifying force. Pinto let out a scream as the tiger's jaws clamped down on his leg.

"No!" Priya screamed, her hands grabbing onto Pinto, trying desperately to pull him up. But the tiger was too strong, dragging him backward with a low growl.

Pinto's screams echoed through the night as the tiger pulled him into the darkness. Blood stained the ground beneath him, and his cries grew fainter until they were swallowed by the jungle.

Priya stood frozen, staring into the darkness where Pinto had disappeared, tears streaming down her face. Her hands were still gripping the bloodied ladder, her knuckles white with the effort.

"Priya!" Siddharth's voice called down from above. "Come on! You have to climb!"

But Priya couldn't move, her body trembling with shock and helplessness. The tiger's glowing green eyes flashed in her mind, and the memory of its golden eyes so calm, so connected to her felt like a distant, unreachable dream.

"Priya, please!" Kritika's voice was desperate now. "We can't lose you too!"

With a shuddering breath, Priya tore her eyes away from the darkness and slowly began to climb, her hands shaking as she pulled herself up the ladder. Tears continued to flow silently down her cheeks as she reached the top, collapsing into Siddharth and Kritika's arms.

Together, they huddled on the platform at the top of the tower, their hearts heavy with the loss of Mr. Pinto. The jungle below them was silent once more, but the haunting memory of the tiger and the terror of what was still out there lingered in the air.

Priya wiped her tears, her voice barely above a whisper. "We have to stop them… No matter what."

Chapter – 8

THE ESCAPE PLAN

The night air at the top of the tower was frigid, but the trio barely noticed as they sat in silence, each wrapped in their own thoughts. Below, the jungle stretched into an endless sea of darkness, broken only by the occasional flicker of moonlight through the trees.

"We're not safe here forever," Siddharth said. "If they control the tiger, they could send it up here or send more guards after us."

Kritika wrapped her arms around her knees, her gaze fixed on the forest floor below. "What do we do? Pinto was our only guide… and now, we're back to square one."

Priya looked at her friends, with stern resolve in her eyes. "We keep going. Pinto sacrificed himself to help us, and we owe it to him to finish this. That man and his accomplice…they need to be stopped."

"But we don't even know who they are," Kritika murmured, shaking her head. "They control that tiger like it's their pet… they treat it like a weapon."

"When the tiger looked at me earlier… I felt something, like it was more than just an animal. It showed me memories, maybe even its own memories of pain and loss… being taken from its family. It's a prisoner too, just like Bill and Margaret. And that man with the remote…

he's turning everything he touches into a pawn for whatever twisted plan he has. We have to do something."

A sudden clang from below startled all three of them as they peered over the edge of the platform. A small team of guards, dressed in black uniforms and carrying flashlights, had reached the base of the tower.

"We have to move. Now," Kritika whispered, her voice barely audible as the flashlights swept closer.

"There's no ladder down the back," Siddharth said, scanning the sides. "They've cornered us."

Priya's mind raced, adrenaline sharpening her senses. "Wait… do you see that tree branch?" She pointed to a thick branch from a nearby tree that stretched just close enough to the tower that they might be able to jump to it. "It's risky, but it's our only shot."

The three shared a look. Siddharth nodded, his jaw set. "Okay. One at a time. I'll go first."

Before Kritika could voice her hesitation, Siddharth gripped the edge of the platform and leapt toward the branch. He caught it, swinging for a terrifying moment before managing to wrap his legs around it, then slowly eased himself along the branch toward the trunk. He turned and gave the girls a nod.

Kritika took a deep breath. "Wish me luck." She gripped the edge of the platform, whispered a quick prayer, and jumped. Her hands grasped the branch, and after a moment of hanging precariously, she crawled along the branch to where Siddharth waited.

Priya's heart pounded as she prepared to make the jump. With one last glance down at the guards circling the base, she leapt, catching the branch and quickly scrambling her way to her friends. They helped her down the trunk until they reached the ground, crouching behind a thick cluster of bushes.

The guards' voices grew louder as they searched the tower. They didn't have much time. The trio slipped quietly through the shadows, moving as silently as possible to avoid being detected.

After what felt like hours of creeping through the jungle, they stopped to catch their breath. Kritika leaned against a tree, wiping her brow. "We need to find a safe place to regroup, somewhere out of their reach."

Priya nodded, scanning the area. "There's that abandoned temple we saw earlier near the resort. It looked secluded and might give us some cover."

Siddharth frowned. "It's risky. They could have patrols nearby. But right now, we don't have many options."

They pressed on, pushing through dense foliage, the temple finally coming into view as dawn began to break. They slipped inside the crumbling structure, huddling in the shadows as they planned their next move.

"We have to send out some kind of signal for help," Kritika whispered. "If we can get word to someone outside, maybe the authorities can come."

Siddharth nodded. "Agreed. But first, we need to understand what exactly we're dealing with. Priya, can you try to remember any details about that man? Anything specific that could help us track down his identity?"

Priya closed her eyes, recalling the chilling look in the man's eyes as he controlled the tiger. "He had this… strange presence, like he was obsessed with the tiger. He called himself the tiger's father, like he was connected to it somehow."

Kritika shivered. "Maybe he sees the tiger as more than just a weapon, as a project he's developed."

Siddharth looked at Priya. "Did you notice anything that could explain how he controls it?"

Priya thought back to the small remote the woman had handed him. "It's definitely some kind of tech. He used a remote to control the tiger, and the moment he pressed it, the tiger just… stopped. It was almost as if he switched it off."

Kritika's eyes widened. "If we could get our hands on that remote, we might be able to free the tiger from his control."

Siddharth's face hardened. "Then that's our plan. We get the remote, and we shut down whatever he's built here. But first, we have to stay alive and make sure they don't find us."

Just then, a rustling sound outside the temple made them all freeze. Priya's heart leapt into her throat as the low growl of the tiger echoed through the walls. The same green-eyed predator that had taken Mr. Pinto was now hunting them.

They scrambled deeper into the temple, ducking behind a collapsed stone pillar as the tiger's shadow slinked into the entrance, It moved silently, the only sound the quiet rumble of its growl as it searched for them.

"Stay absolutely still," Siddharth whispered, his voice barely audible.

The tiger prowled closer, its keen eyes narrowing as it sensed their presence. Priya squeezed her eyes shut, her heart hammering in her chest as the beast approached. But just when it seemed they were doomed, a loud crack rang out - a gunshot. The tiger flinched, turning its head toward the source of the sound.

Footsteps echoed as the guards entered the temple, "Where is it? Find the tiger, and take care of those intruders!"

The tiger's gaze locked onto the guards, and with a sudden, explosive burst of speed, it lunged at them, its claws tearing through the air. The guards screamed, their rifles falling from their hands as the tiger tore into them with a fierce, unrestrained fury.

"Now's our chance!" Siddharth hissed, grabbing Priya and Kritika by the arms. The three friends darted through a side entrance, slipping out into the jungle.

They didn't stop running, weaving through the dense foliage until they reached a small clearing where they finally stopped, gasping for breath.

Chapter – 9

INTO THE HEART OF DARKNESS

The sun was just beginning to rise, casting streaks of gold through the dense canopy above as Priya, Siddharth, and Kritika moved stealthily through the jungle. Though their hearts were pounding, a shared determination pushed them forward, their focus fixed on one goal: finding the lab and exposing the people who had taken control of both the tiger and the missing tourists.

The jungle was quiet, as if the wildlife sensed the tension and chose to remain hidden. Each step was deliberate and cautious. They knew that every shadow could be an enemy, every sound a signal of approaching danger.

Siddharth broke the silence, his voice barely a whisper. "The lab has to be close. We're retracing the path those guards took back from the temple, so it must be deeper in."

Priya nodded, glancing nervously around. "Let's hope we find it before they find us."

As they trekked through the dense vegetation, Kritika gestured to a narrow path lined with odd, freshly disturbed patches of earth. She leaned closer to inspect the ground. "Looks like these are tire marks. Could be from vehicles transporting their equipment."

They followed the tire marks, quickening their pace but careful not to leave any signs of their own trail. The thick underbrush finally opened to reveal a large, bunker-like structure, half-hidden under camouflaging vines and moss. High fences surrounded the perimeter, and two guards paced in front of the entrance, rifles slung over their shoulders.

Kritika let out a quiet gasp. "There it is."

Priya crouched low behind a nearby tree, her eyes narrowed. "So, what's our plan? We can't exactly just waltz in."

Siddharth's face was grim as he scanned the area. "We'll need to create a diversion. I'll go first, sneak closer, and try to get inside while you two cover me."

Priya nodded. "We'll be ready to follow as soon as you're in. Be careful."

He flashed them a reassuring grin. "I'll be fine. Just keep an eye out." With that, he moved swiftly and silently toward the perimeter, sticking close to the shadows until he was right by the fence.

Kritika looked over at Priya, worry etched on her face. "Do you think he'll make it?"

"He has to," Priya replied, though her voice betrayed her own doubt. They kept their eyes fixed on Siddharth's figure as he neared a gap in the fencing where two sections were poorly fastened. Just as he began to squeeze through, the guards turned in his direction, squinting suspiciously into the trees.

"Now!" Priya whispered, grabbing a nearby rock and hurling it toward the other side of the compound. The rock crashed through the underbrush, drawing the guards' attention. Both guards rushed toward the sound, giving Siddharth just enough time to slip through the fence.

With bated breath, Priya and Kritika waited until Siddharth waved them over. They quickly joined him on the other side of the fence, hearts pounding as they pressed their backs against the cool metal of the building's exterior.

They moved along the wall, searching for an entrance, when they heard muffled voices. Peeking around the corner, they saw the same man who claimed to be the tiger's "father" and the woman with the remote. They were standing near a large cage, where the tiger lay unconscious, its body rising and falling in shallow breaths.

"The sedation should last another twelve hours," the woman said, examining the tiger with a critical eye.

The man nodded, his voice cold. "Good. The developers arrive tonight, and we can't risk any unexpected surprises. It's critical that we have the jungle empty of tourists by then."

Priya's stomach churned with anger and revulsion. Empty of tourists? Did they plan to kill them all? She clenched her fists, fighting the urge to rush forward and confront them, but Siddharth held her back.

"Wait," he whispered, his gaze fixed on the woman as she took out a tablet and began typing on it.

"We'll control the tiger remotely for now," she continued, "It's too dangerous to trust the animal's instincts. The guards might have to intervene to carry out the killings."

The man smirked. "You're right. But don't forget, we also have to make the deaths look like animal attacks. Our clients expect it."

Kritika covered her mouth to stifle a gasp. She looked at the others, horror etched across her face. "They're planning to kill us too? Like Pinto?"

Siddharth's jaw tightened, his eyes narrowed with fury. "They're monsters. But now we know what they're doing… we just have to figure out how to stop it."

"We'll be out of this jungle by sunrise tomorrow, leaving behind nothing but legends…" said the man as he let out a sinister chuckle, sending a chill down Priya's spine. She exchanged a determined glance with Siddharth and Kritika, her eyes blazing with resolve.

"This ends tonight," she whispered fiercely.

But just as they began formulating a plan, a twig snapped underfoot. All three froze, but it was too late; the woman's head whipped around, her eyes narrowing.

"Who's there?" she demanded, her hand slipping to her belt where a sleek black pistol hung.

Without thinking, Siddharth whispered, "Run!" They bolted, darting back through the jungle.

"Guards! Over there, in the trees!"

Heavy footsteps pursued them as they sprinted through the thick underbrush, dodging branches and jumping over roots. The jungle blurred around them as adrenaline coursed through their veins, their only goal to put as much distance as possible between themselves and their pursuers.

Suddenly, a loud roar filled the air, freezing them in their tracks. The tiger, no longer unconscious, had awakened, and its eyes glowed a furious green as it prowled through the compound.

Siddharth pushed Priya and Kritika forward. "Go! It's coming!"

They broke into a full sprint, the sound of paws thudding against the ground growing louder behind them. The jungle seemed endless, and every step felt like a race against death itself.

Ahead, the dark outline of a cliff's edge appeared, the forest falling away to reveal a sheer drop into the misty depths below.

"We're trapped!" Kritika gasped, looking around desperately.

Siddharth looked back, then at the cliff. "There's only one way out of this."

Priya's heart pounded as she realized what he meant. "Jump?"

"There seems to be a water body down below. It's the only choice we have!" he said, his eyes fierce with determination.

Priya looked back at the tiger, its form stalking closer, its green eyes locked onto them. She took a deep breath, steeling herself.

"Together, then," she said, reaching for Siddharth and Kritika's hands.

The three friends looked at each other one last time, a silent pact passing between them. Then, without hesitation, they leapt off the cliff, plunging into the misty abyss as the tiger's roar echoed above them.

Chapter – 10

THE PROTECTOR AWAKENS

The world spun as Priya, Siddharth, and Kritika plunged through the mist, the wind howling in their ears. They hit the water with a shocking jolt! The cool rush swallowed them whole, breaking their fall and pulling them under for a moment before they kicked toward the surface.

Priya broke through gasping for air as droplets streamed down her face. She spotted Siddharth coughing nearby and Kritika swimming toward the shore, her braid trailing behind like a water snake. They had landed in a wide, hidden pool tucked beneath the cliff, fed by a narrow stream that trickled down the rocks.

All around them, jungle vines hung low over the water, and tall trees leaned in like quiet guardians.

"Is everyone okay?" Siddharth called, wiping water from his eyes as he paddled closer to the shore.

"Barely," Kritika said, breathless as she dragged herself onto a mossy rock. "But we're alive. That was insane."

Priya nodded, scanning the shadows. The realization of their narrow escape sank in, but relief was fleeting. The low growl of the tiger echoed from somewhere nearby, sending chills through them.

Suddenly, a rustling in the bushes made them freeze. The tiger emerged, with gleaming green eyes.

But something in its stance was different, it was no longer prowling with aggression but instead stood alert, watching them carefully. For a tense moment, the three friends stared into its eyes, expecting another attack.

But the tiger didn't move to strike. Instead, it lowered its head, as though in thought. Then, with a low rumble, its eyes flashed - golden, like molten sunlight and a strange calm settled over them.

"That's… it's the same eyes," Priya whispered, unable to tear her gaze away. "The golden eyes I saw before."

Siddharth and Kritika exchanged puzzled glances. The tiger stepped forward, this time exuding a sense of power that was awe-inspiring rather than threatening. It seemed almost protective, like a guardian standing between them and the jungle's dangers. With a slow, deliberate glance over its shoulder and a flick of its tail, it began to walk away, pausing just long enough to be sure they were watching.

"I think it wants us to follow it," Siddharth murmured, his voice low with wonder.

Moving in sync, they followed the tiger as it led them through the thick jungle. The path it took was unfamiliar but filled with a strange energy. Priya felt a sense of reverence, as if they were walking in sacred territory.

All around them, the forest shimmered with life. Moss glowed faintly on ancient tree trunks, and butterflies with iridescent wings flitted through beams of golden light that pierced the canopy. The air buzzed with the gentle hum of unseen insects, while vibrant birds with jeweled feathers darted overhead, calling out in musical tones like a chorus from some hidden world.

A pair of curious langurs watched from a branch, tails curled like question marks, while fireflies blinked between the leaves even though the sun had not yet set. The jungle didn't feel wild, it felt alive, aware, almost protective.

With every step, it became harder to tell whether they were still in the real world… or had crossed into something ancient and magical.

After a while, the forest opened into a clearing, revealing a hidden grove surrounded by towering ancient trees. The air was different here, alive and tingling with the presence of something larger than themselves. The tiger moved to the center of the grove and turned to face them, its golden eyes reflecting the glow of the first morning light.

"It's as if… it's as if it's protecting this place," Kritika whispered, her eyes wide with awe.

Priya stepped forward, her heart thundering. "This tiger… it's more than an animal. I think it's the protector of this jungle."

The tiger lowered its gaze, and Priya felt a strange connection wash over her, stronger than before. Suddenly, the tiger's eyes filled with images, and a vision unfolded in her mind. She saw the tiger as it once was - a free, powerful creature roaming the jungle with its family. But then she saw the man with the remote, his greed, his determination to use the tiger as a weapon to control the forest. She saw tourists captured, caged, and killed only to be used as examples of how dangerous this place was. And then, the last image, a vision of the tiger, breaking free from the remote's hold and standing as a defender of the jungle.

As the vision faded, Priya's heart filled with understanding. She looked at Siddharth and Kritika. "The legends… they're real. This tiger is the vessel for the deity, the protector of this place. It's here to save the jungle… and us."

"So… it was never just an animal. It was always meant to protect this land, no matter who tried to control it." said Siddharth.

Kritika nodded, her eyes wet with unshed tears. "The deity's spirit, the tiger deity… it's alive, in this tiger."

Just then, a sharp crackle echoed from the jungle behind them. Flashlights bobbed in the distance, and the voices of the guards grew louder as they closed in. The three friends turned back to the tiger, fear gripping them again.

But the tiger stepped forward, positioning itself between them and the approaching guards. Its golden eyes narrowed with fierce determination, and a low, rumbling growl filled the air. The jungle seemed to come alive with its energy, as if all of nature were rising to protect its protector.

The guards emerged from the underbrush, guns raised, but the tiger let out an earth-shaking roar that echoed through the trees. Birds took flight, animals scattered, and the ground seemed to tremble. The guards faltered, their eyes wide with terror.

"Open fire!" one of them shouted, raising his weapon.

But before they could pull their triggers, the ground beneath them gave a sudden, thunderous shudder. With a deep, cracking sound, the earth split open. The forest floor crumbled beneath the guards' feet, and they let out cries of shock as they tumbled into the darkness below, swallowed by the jungle itself.

The tiger halted at the edge, and let out a roar that echoed through the trees. It turned back to the three friends. Stepping closer, its fierce expression softened, and with a last look at them - a look that held understanding and a shared purpose - it padded back into the depths of the jungle, blending into the shadows until it disappeared completely.

Priya, Siddharth, and Kritika stood there, the weight of the experience sinking in. The silence in the grove felt peaceful now, no longer filled with fear or danger. They knew, with certainty, that the jungle was safe.

Siddharth broke the silence, his voice hushed with reverence. "I never thought I'd believe in something like this… a protector, a deity."

Priya smiled, her heart filled with a mix of sadness and awe. "The tiger deity… it saved us. It saved this jungle. And in some way, it's still here, watching over everything."

Just then a nearby banyan tree rustled vigorously. All three friends turned sharply as the roots of the tree began to shift, parting slightly above a small, narrow hole hidden in the undergrowth. Leaves fluttered as three familiar figures emerged one by one, blinking against the dappled light.

"Bill?" Priya gasped.

"And Margaret!" Kritika cried.

"You're alive!" said Priya before jumping in to hug them with tears of joy in her eyes.

Last to climb out was Mr. Pinto, brushing dirt from his coat and looking thoroughly bewildered.

"We thought you were gone!" Siddharth exclaimed, rushing over.

Margaret smiled, her face smudged with soil. "Not quite."

Bill nodded toward the tree. "The tiger led us through an underground clearing," he said, his voice steady but laced with awe. "We didn't know where it was taking us, but it never hurt us. It even dragged Mr. Pinto after it knocked him out cold, guess it figured he needed a wake-up call."

Mr. Pinto gave a sheepish shrug.

"We heard voices above," Bill continued, "so we followed the sound… and here we are."

Priya stared at the opening in the ground, then back at the now-quiet jungle. "It brought us all here… on purpose."

"We were lucky today," said Kritka. "But what happens tomorrow? What if more people come? What if they send more guards… more machines?"

Bill glanced toward the hole they had emerged from, his brow furrowed. "They will. Places like this… they're always in danger. Someone always wants to own it, pave it, profit from it."

Priya's voice wavered, her eyes fierce. "This jungle, it's sacred. We've seen it. Felt it. It's alive. But no one out there will believe us."

Mr. Pinto cleared his throat, drawing their attention. "There's something I need to show you," he said, reaching into his pocket. "While I was lying down there, in that hole beneath the tree, before I fully came to, I felt something pressed against my side. It must've been buried in the dirt or dropped during the chaos."

He pulled out a small object and held it up.

It was a silver memory drive, scratched and slightly bent, its metallic surface dulled by dust and age. In faded black ink, scrawled across one side, were the words: "PROJECT TIGER."

The group leaned in, wide-eyed.

"It must've fallen in during the scuffle," Pinto said, turning it over in his hand. "Maybe when one of the guards tackled me. Or…" he looked at Priya. "Maybe the tiger wanted me to have it."

Priya blinked. "What's on it?"

"Hopefully proof," Siddharth said, taking a closer look. "Evidence. Plans. Something we can show the world."

Pinto nodded, a quiet resolve setting into his features. "If this contains what I think it does, detailed operations, names, funding trails, we'll have the leverage we need. These people… they won't be able to hide behind permits and paperwork anymore."

Kritika leaned closer. "Do you think it'll be enough?"

"It has to be," Pinto said firmly. "I'll take this to the authorities. Real ones. Environmental protection agencies, media outlets, anyone who is willing to listen. And if they won't act… I will. I'll make sure this jungle stays untouched."

For a long moment, no one spoke. Then Priya slowly stood and looked around at the grove, the trees swaying as if in quiet agreement.

"This place gave us its trust," she said softly. "Now we have to protect it, even if the world doesn't understand why."

As the morning sun climbed higher, the group began their slow walk out of the grove, hearts full, minds racing. They didn't know what the future would bring, but they knew the jungle wasn't alone anymore.

The jungle now felt alive with the spirit of the tiger. The ancient legends weren't just stories; they were real, etched into the fabric of the jungle and embodied in the tiger that had fought to protect them. They had witnessed something beyond explanation, a bond between the wilderness and a protector that transcended time.

And though they left the jungle behind, they knew they carried with them a story, a truth, and a connection to a power older and greater than themselves; a power that would continue to guard the jungle long after they were gone.

--- **To be continued** ---